EMMA JUST MEDIUM:

"I can't get enough of Emma and her whole family! Emma is goofy, well-intentioned, and one hundred percent relatable— all the more when she makes mistakes. Her family and friends radiate love for one another. Kids who adore *Clementine*, *Judy Moody*, and Sharon Draper's *Sassy* will delight in this story of a spunky girl doing everything she can to create space for herself in her family."

– Rebecca Fox, Asst Manager of Family Services,
New Canaan, CT, Library

EMMA JUST MEDIUM:

Laura Wiltse Prior

with illustrations by Marta Kissi

ONE ELM
BOOKS

Egremont, Massachusetts

One Elm Books is an imprint of Red Chair Press LLC

Red Chair Press LLC   PO Box 333   South Egremont, MA 01258-0333

www.redchairpress.com

Free Discussion Guide available online.

To Joe, my teammate

–LWP

Publisher's Cataloging-In-Publication Data
Names: Prior, Laura Wiltse, author. | Kissi, Marta, illustrator.

Title: Emma Just Medium. The beach dilemma / Laura Wiltse Prior, with illustrations by Marta Kissi.

Other Titles: Beach dilemma

Description: Egremont, Massachusetts : One Elm Books, [2023] | Series: Emma Just Medium ; [1] | Interest age level: 007-010. | Summary: "Even though her family calls her Emma Bemma, Emma knows she is really just Medium. That's because she's the middle kid between her two brothers, who everyone calls Big and Little. Big thinks he's the coolest kid on the planet now that he's 10. And everyone thinks Little is just adorable even when he picks his nose and eats it! What if she could get out of being the middle by taking on a new role? What if she acted BIG? Or even bigger than that?"-- Provided by publisher.

Identifiers: ISBN 9781947159600 (hardcover) | ISBN 9781947159617 (ePDF) | ISBN 9781947159624 (ePub 3 S&L) | ISBN 9781947159631 (ePub 3 TR) | ISBN 9781947159648 (Kindle)

Subjects: LCSH: Middle-born children--Juvenile fiction. | Brothers and sisters--Juvenile fiction. | Identity (Psychology) in children--Juvenile fiction. | Beaches--Juvenile fiction. | CYAC: Middle-born children--Fiction. | Brothers and sisters--Fiction. | Identity--Fiction. | Beaches--Fiction.

Classification: LCC PZ7.1.P768 Em 2023 (print) | LCC PZ7.1.P768 (ebook) | DDC [E]--dc23

LC record available at https://lccn.loc.gov/2022935632
Main body text set in Baskerville 16/23
Text copyright Laura Wiltse Prior
Copyright © 2024 Red Chair Press LLC

Printed in the United States of America

0523 1P CGF23

Table of Contents

CHAPTER 1

Emma's Dilemma

Emma cuddled in bed with Emmaphant. She listened to the raindrops plop outside. Today her family was driving to a beach vacation with the Farber family. Just like every year.

"Let's go! Let's go!" rang from the hallway.

Emma giggled. Her dad made up silly songs for everything. She knew what came next.

"Let's start the show!" she sang back.

"All the boys, gather your toys!" Dad called, keeping the tune going.

"I don't have toys anymore, Dad, I'm ten!" a voice yelled, ruining the song. It was Emma's older brother, who everyone called 'Big'. Big used to sing along with Dad. He didn't do that anymore. Lately he was too old for lots of stuff that Emma still liked.

"Daddy, get may toys!" shouted Emma's younger brother, whose nickname was 'Little'. Little wanted to play with Emma sometimes, but he was too young to understand most of her games. He mostly knocked things over.

That was the thing that bothered Emma. Big and Little's nicknames described them perfectly. Emma's nickname was different. Probably because everyone felt bad calling her 'Just Medium' or 'Middle'. Emma knew that was who she was anyway.

"Emma Bemma, be a star, while your father packs the car," Dad rhymed, walking into her room. He wore his yellow starfish shirt, the one he always wore for a beach vacation.

Emma rolled out of bed. She put on the clothing

she picked out the night before—green shorts, green socks and a green shirt. It was too bad that when she said "green" it came out like "gween" no matter how much she practiced. Big always made fun of her for it. It would have been much easier if blue was her favorite color.

Next she turned to her Siamese fighting fish, Special, Star and Silly. They lived in three separate tanks. Otherwise, they would attack each other. Emma straightened the instructions she'd written in green crayon to Granny and Grandpa. 'Feed a pinch once a day, talk to each fish for five minutes.'

"Adios," she whispered to her fish. "That's Spanish for goodbye," she added. Emma learned a lot of Spanish in the first grade. She had to practice if she wanted to remember it for second grade.

"Be extra nice to Special," she added to Star and Silly. Special's tank was the middle. Emma knew that the middle could be an extra hard place to be.

Then she snapped her fingers open and shut to

say goodbye in the special crab wave. She and her friend, Wes the Best, invented the wave on vacation last year. She was pretty sure that Special waved his fin back at her.

Emma's stomach panged a bit. She would really miss her fish. But she was excited to see Wes. He was a middle too so he liked the same things Emma did. They always had lots of fun together.

"Emma Bemma!" came a voice from down the hall. "Don't forget to brush your teeth and hair!"

"Ok, Mommy!"

Emma ran a toothbrush over her teeth. Then she picked up the brush. She looked in the mirror. Her hair stood up in different directions. That was just how she liked it. She put the brush right back down.

Emma grabbed the soccer duffel bag she had packed up the night before. Then she opened the door.

CRASH! WAAA!

Little lay crying at her feet.

"Big!" Emma said. "Mommy said never carry Little on your back! And, you're supposed to be getting ready!" The boys never listened.

"Emma Bemma you're not the boss!" said Big.

"Emma Bemma no bas! Emma Bemma no bas!" shouted Little.

Sometimes Emma wished she had a separate place to live from her brothers, just like Special did.

She stepped over the pile of boys. Just as she did, Little stuck his leg out. Emma tripped. She landed in the middle of her brothers.

"Owww!" yelled Emma.

"Emma Bemma hurt may!" shouted Little.

"Are you ok, Little?" asked Big.

"What about me?" cried Emma.

"Everyone into the car!" called Mommy. Emma

tried to get up. She was stuck. Right between the boys. She wiped a trickle from her eye. Being a middle was going to ruin vacation. Just like last year. Emma felt her angry face come out, the one she practiced in the mirror sometimes with her eyebrows scrunched together and her nose crinkled up. She turned to Big.

"You are a Big Bully!"

Then she looked to Little, "And you are Little Meany! Those are your new nicknames!"

That made Emma feel a little better. She squirmed out of the pile and headed out to the car. The boys' laughter chased after her.

7

CHAPTER 2

Emma Just Medium

When she got to the car, Emma found out where she was sitting.

The Middle. Again!

"Why do I always have to be in the middle?" she asked her parents.

"You know why, Emma Bemma," Dad and Mommy said together.

She did know why. Her booster seat fit just right between Little's car seat and Big's larger body. It still wasn't fair.

Dad weaved the car through the town streets. He zipped onto the highway. Water went splat on the windshield.

Big moved his legs into Emma's space.

"Mommy! He's crossing the line!" Emma said, tracing the invisible divider with her finger.

"It's not my fault! I'm having a growth spurt!" said Big, grinning.

Emma examined her own legs. They tucked into the space between the cooler and the beach blanket easily. She looked at Mommy's. They were cross-legged in the front seat. Mommy was good at that because she taught yoga. A big brown bag full of snacks took up all the room at her feet.

Emma decided to sit like Mommy.

"Move your knee," said Big. He shoved it right back down.

"Mommy!" Emma shouted. Mommy closed her eyes for a second. That was another yoga thing.

"Work it out, you two," she said, opening her eyes again. "Communicate."

Emma wasn't sure what 'communicate' meant. She turned back to Big. He was already playing on his dumb iPad. That's all he did since he got one for his tenth birthday.

"Don't play that. You'll throw up again!" Emma exclaimed. When it rained, you could smell Big's thrown-up breakfast from the last time. And it was raining right now. Gross!

"Don't tell me what to do," said Big.

"He's not listening!" said Emma.

"That's not what I meant by working it out, Emma," sighed Mommy.

"Can I have my own iPad?" Emma tried. She knew the answer already.

"You're too young," said Big.

"Big…," warned Dad.

"What?" Big said, smiling and raising his hands up in the air. "It's true!"

"When we gonna be theya?" Little asked for the billionth time.

"We've only been in the car for ten minutes Little," said Big in a special voice that sounded like syrup. "We've got a looong way to go."

Emma felt tears returning to her eyes.

"Mommy!" she said. "Big is *always* nice to Little. But not to me!" The tears began to burst through.

"Let's all take a deep cleansing breathe together," said Mommy.

"I don't want to!" Emma shouted.

"You have to breathe to live, Emma Bemma," said Big.

"Big, that's enough," said Mommy. She reached back and patted Emma's knee. It felt good. It would be better if she could sit in Mommy's lap. Little took that spot most of the time nowadays. Emma tried to look out the windows but both views were blocked by brothers.

"Let's try a song!" Dad said. Emma knew he was trying to cheer everyone up. She didn't want to.

"Ohhhhhh, row row row your boat," Dad started to sing, waiting for the family to join in. Only Little did. And he got the words wrong.

For lunch, they went to a drive-thru restaurant.

"I hate burgers!" said Emma.

"Can you at least try one?" pleaded Dad. "This is the only restaurant for miles."

"I won't eat anything!" Emma declared.

"How about one of these?" Mommy reached into her big brown bag. She held up a brown, squishy banana, a pack of crumbly crackers and a mushy cheese stick.

"No, gracias," said Emma. It came out 'gacias'.

"You're not Spanish, Emma," said Big.

"Gacias! Gacias!" shouted Little.

"It's gracias!" said Emma, but it came out the same way as it did for Little.

Emma turned her angry face to Big, then to Little, then back to Big again. It started to hurt her mouth. She had to take a break.

This was the worst drive ever.

After lunch, Emma's belly growled. She ate the brown banana. She did not like it.

Little fell asleep. His sweaty head slumped on

Emma's shoulder. Big went back to his iPad.

"Put it down," said Dad. Dad knew exactly what was happening in the back seat. That's what the mirror on the windshield was for.

Little opened his eyes.

"Aww we theya?" he cried.

"Be quiet…," Emma started to yell, but Big made a yucky sound next to her. The next second, Emma felt wet slime dripping down her head.

"Big!" screamed Emma, wiping her big brother's throw-up out of her eyes.

"I'm sick! It's not my fault!" Big cried.

"Pull over!" Mommy commanded.

"We're on the highway!" Dad shouted.

Mommy reached back with greasy lunch napkins. She tried to wipe Emma's face. Instead she spread the slime into her hair. Emma pushed her hands away.

"Aww we theya?" asked Little.

That was enough. Emma shouted straight at

Little's face, "IT'S THERE, NOT THEYA! AND NO WE ARE NOT THERE!"

Little's brown eyes turned extra big like a cartoon character. His mouth formed a little 'O'. He started to cry.

"Emma Bemma!" yelled Mommy and Dad at the same time.

"He's only three," scolded Dad.

"He doesn't understand. He's little," said Mommy.

Emma sunk into her gloppy seat.

After that, Dad found a rest stop. Mommy cleaned Emma up. She smoothed her hair. When Mommy turned around, Emma messed it up again.

The car was even stinkier than before.

Dad spoke in his special voice again, "Ok crew! Let's think of all the fun we're going to have with the Farbers!"

"Yeah, Sara and I have been texting each other with plans," said Big.

"Can I know the plans?" asked Emma.

"Sorry, they're for big kids," said Big.

Emma's stomach twisted. She wanted a plan too.

"I have pwans!" yelled Little. Emma knew Little's plans. He would knock down her sandcastles. He would cry about everything. And worst of all, he was mean to the beach creatures that Emma collected and cared for. Last year, he almost crushed a hermit crab!

Everyone kept talking. No one noticed that Emma was quiet. She was thinking about how this vacation would turn out just like everything else did. All because she wasn't big. Or small. Emma Bemma was Emma Just Medium.

This vacation was going to be a real dil*Emma*. That was the word Mommy used when there was a problem.

If only everyone forgot she was just medium, things might be different.

Emma sat up with a jolt. That was it! She would switch things up on this vacation. She would act like she'd been born in a different order!

Now Emma had her very own plan. Why hadn't she thought of this before?

The rest of the car trip went by in a flash.

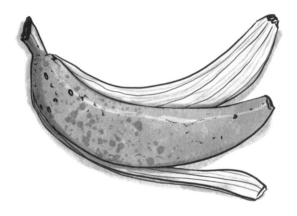

CHAPTER 3

Lego® and Magnets

"Emma Bemma, your little friend is waiting for you…" Big sang as they pulled up to the beach house hours later.

"I'm not little!" Emma protested. But she also felt a wave of excitement. Wes the Best was standing on the front porch. His blond hair looked like it had been through a tornado. He opened and closed both of his hands with the special crab wave at the same time.

Dad shut off the engine. As the rest of Wes's family came pouring out of the house, Emma realized something bad. If she wasn't going to be medium, she didn't match up with other mediums anymore. And that's what Wes the Best was—the middle between his sisters Sara and Baby Beth. Emma had a new dil*Emma*.

Mommy got out. She unbuckled Little from his car seat. She gave the Farber parents a hug. Then she turned back to the car.

"What's wrong Emma Bemma?" she asked. Emma wasn't climbing out from the middle seat. Her tummy swished like a washing machine.

"I can't play with Wes," Emma whispered.

Mommy cocked her head.

"What do you mean?" said Mommy. "You always play with him."

Emma realized she sounded very middle. She tried again.

"I would prefer not to play with Wesley this year, Madame," said Emma. Yes, that sounded very big, just like people in some of the TV shows Mommy and Dad watched at night.

"Emma Bemma, why are you speaking with a British accent?" Mommy asked.

"I'm not," said Emma. "And I'm not Emma Bemma anymore. Just Emma."

"Ok, Mademoiselle Emma," said Mommy, raising her eyebrows. "Just be nice to Wes, please. You've been friends since you were tiny babies."

Mommy reached in to give Emma a hand out of the car. She tucked Emma's hair behind her ear. Emma moved to take it right back out. Then she realized that was a very middle thing to do. A big person would wear her hair neatly. She tucked it back again and did the other side too.

Emma grabbed her bag of LEGO® bricks from the trunk. Then she remembered that playing LEGO® was not a big thing to do. She tossed the bag back into the car. It opened up. Rainbow pieces sprinkled all over the seats and floor.

A moist hand gripped her arm.

"Emma Bemma!" Wes the Best shouted in her ear. Emma wanted to jump up and down. She wanted to do the special crab wave. She knew she couldn't.

"Hello Wesley," she said. She leaned in and kissed the air right next to his cheek. Big people always gave hello kisses like that.

"Awwww," sighed Mrs. Farber. She took a picture with her phone.

"We can use it on their wedding day!" said Mommy.

"I'm not ever getting marr…!" Emma started to say. Then she stopped. Big people got married… a lot!

Then Sara zipped right passed Emma. Straight over to Big.

"Oh, those two are like magnets," smiled Mommy. Emma learned about magnets in science class. They were always pulled towards each other. Just like Big and Sara. They moved to their own corner of the yard. Sara talked. Big grinned. He nodded his head up and down like the dancing dinosaur Little watched on TV. They were probably working on their plans.

Emma tried to swallow. Her throat was stuck shut. Big used to be Emma's very best friend. They would create forts out of the couch cushions. They would build LEGO® pirate ships together. They could even have fun just talking and walking.

But ever since Big got to fourth grade, things were different. Now he looked at Emma like she was the last person on Earth he wanted to see. It made Emma's heart squeeze thinking of it.

"Emma Bemma," said Wes, reappearing beside her. "I picked these up for you! Let's play!" Emma looked. He held a pile of her LEGO® bricks with dirty hands. All of a sudden Wes seemed very loud. And messy. She realized he was very middle.

"I'm Emma now," she corrected, "and I don't…" But Wes had already wrapped a sticky hand around her wrist.

22

The plan to be big wasn't working yet. Emma needed to be even bigger. She started to figure out the details as Wes pulled her towards the house.

CHAPTER 4

Later, at the beach, Emma searched through her backpack for the secret items she had taken from Mommy's suitcase.

Wes sat close to her.

"Wanna dig a big hole?" he asked. For a second Emma wanted to say yes. But that would mess everything up.

"I can't. I'm working on a plan," she said. Emma already felt bigger just saying that.

Emma studied the big kids. Sara moved her hands around a lot. She whispered something in Big's ear. They were planning something. Something big. Emma needed to be a part of it.

"Can I be a part of the plan?" said Wes.

"Sorry," said Emma, shaking her head, "it's top secret."

Wes considered that.

"Well, wanna build a sandcastle?" he tried.

"No, gracias," said Emma.

"What does that mean?" Wes asked. Emma rolled her eyes. Wes didn't even know Spanish.

Her fingers found what they'd been searching for. Emma pulled it out of the bag. She swiped it over her lips. A small chunk slipped into her mouth. Yuck! It tasted like crayons.

"You're not old enough for lipstick," said Wes.

"That's what you think," Emma said.

Wes cocked his head sideways. Then he said, "Wanna go swimming?"

"No!" said Emma. Why did he keep asking? She moved a little bit away from him. He moved with her.

Emma pulled out the sarong she found in Mommy's suitcase earlier, the one with the yoga symbols on it. The sarong seemed magical. Mommy wore it a different way every day. Sometimes it was a skirt, sometimes a scarf and sometimes even a headband! Emma wrapped the magic sarong under her arms. She turned and turned until she was wrapped like a mummy.

"What are you doing Emma Bemma?" asked Wes.

"Just Emma!" she hissed. Then she put Mommy's straw hat on her head. It slid down her face.

"Can you see?" asked Wes.

Emma didn't answer. The big kids were just sitting together on the beach towel. Big was grinning. At nothing. Being big looked super boring. But Emma knew she had to do the same thing.

She shifted in the direction of Super Sara and Big. The sarong was slipping down. Being big was so uncomfortable. Emma dragged herself along.

She was almost at Big and Sara's blanket.

"Emma! Come sit with us!" said Big. He patted the spot in front of him. Emma tried to step onto the beach blanket. The sarong was too long. Emma tripped on the extra material.

OH NO! She was falling.

Then she was down. Way, way down.

Big and Sara were laughing.

"It worked! It worked!" Big snorted.

"What worked?" Emma yelled, smacking the hat off her head.

"Our epic trap! We dug a deep hole. Then we covered it with the blanket. You fell right into it!"

"Big Bully!" Emma shrieked. "Stupid Sara!"

She knew they'd been planning something!

"Nice lipstick," Big said, as he pointed at her and slapped his knees.

Emma wished she would sink all the way down to the middle of the earth. But then she would be stuck in the middle. Again!

"Are you ok Emma Bemma?" Wes was looking down at Emma.

"No!" She crawled out of the hole. She threw

Mommy's dumb clothing in a pile and ran away. Wes caught up to her.

"I fell in a mud hole once," he said. "I ate some of the mud. It tasted like wet dirt." Wes sounded like such a middle.

"I want to be alone," Emma said as she walked away. She sat down by the water and traced her fingers in the sand.

"Look who's awaaake!" called Mrs. Farber from back on the beach. Emma turned around. Mrs. Farber carefully took Baby Beth out from the beach tent where she'd been napping. Beth was the only one who could cheer Emma up right now. She always held Emma's finger. She smelled like vanilla cake mix, the kind Emma's Mommy made for her birthday. Yum. Emma wanted to play with Baby Beth all day long.

Mrs. Farber put Baby Beth on the blanket. Beth glanced around. She saw Emma. She started crawling to her. Emma walked up to meet her. The baby put her hands up. She wanted Emma to hold her! This was Emma's big chance to be bigger! Emma reached down.

"Thanks Emma Bemma, I've got her," said Mrs. Farber, swooping in and grabbing the baby. Emma wouldn't drop Baby Beth. She knew she wouldn't. But no one else believed she wasn't Emma Just Medium.

Emma trudged back to the ocean. This plan was going to be harder than she thought.

A school of fish swam by. They made her think of Star, Special and Sunshine all by themselves. She wanted to be home with them. Emma felt a poke at her back. She turned.

"I got you a present," Wes said. He brought his hand out from behind his back. He handed her a tiny hermit crab.

It was a weird gift. Emma liked it. She tried not to smile.

CHAPTER 5

Creatures and Crayons

That night Emma's family went to a restaurant with the Farbers. White cloths covered the tables. Candles and flowers were everywhere. The smells made her sneeze.

A lady in high heels led them to a round table. Wes took the seat next to Emma. He moved his chair close. This time it was ok. She wasn't trying to be big anymore.

Mommy put Little in a booster seat on the other side of Emma. He stuck his finger up his nostril.

"Why does he have to sit next to me?" Emma asked.

"The big kids wanted some quiet time to themselves," said Mommy as she pulled Little's finger out of his nose. She swiped his hand with a wipe from her purse.

Emma looked at Big and Super Sara across the table. Sara had her hand cupped over her mouth. They were planning again.

"Wes and I want to plan something by ourselves!" said Emma.

"Well, how about planning an amazing picture?" said Mommy, looking over Emma's shoulder. Emma turned. A waitress carried a stack of paper menus and a brimming jar of crayons in every color.

Emma did want to draw something special.

"I'm going to make a magical sea creature!" Emma announced. She could already picture its green and purple scales.

"I'll help you!" said Wes the Best. It was nice to be middle again, for now. Drawing with Wes the Best was always fun.

Emma selected the green crayon.

"THAT MY KAYON!" screeched Little.

"It's my favorite color!" Emma gripped the green crayon tightly.

"GEEN!!" Little screamed. Emma held her hands over her ears.

"Emma, honey, can you please give it to him?" asked Mommy.

"I had it first…" Emma protested.

"Do you want to listen to this the whole meal?" Mommy clutched the table. She looked scared. Little made her look that way sometimes.

"Just give it to him, Emma," said Big. "Coloring is for babies anyway."

Emma plunked down the green crayon. Her head slumped down.

"Don't ruin it for the little kids," pleaded Dad to Big.

"But I'm not little," Emma said. But no one could hear her over Little shouting.

"I NEED GEEN!"

Emma yelled back, "It's green, not geen!" It came out like 'gween'. She caught Dad looking at her. He raised an eyebrow. Emma pretended she didn't see him.

Emma felt like she could burst. She picked up the green crayon. She threw it right at Little. It hit him on the forehead. Oops! Her body tightened. Little was going to scream.

"Emma Bemma!" scolded Mommy.

"He's only three," said Dad.

"You in twubel, Emma Bemma!" shouted Little. He picked up the crayon. He threw it back at Emma. Too hard.

BONK!

It hit a man at the next table on the nose. PLOP! It fell into his bowl. Red soup splashed across the white tablecloth. The people at the table shrieked. They looked around.

Now Little was going to get in trouble!

Emma's parents looked like they'd seen a ghost.

"Sorry, sorry!" they babbled. They jumped out of their seats.

"He's hungry," said Dad.

"He's tired," said Mommy.

Little shook his thick curls around. He waved to the other table. He blew kisses. Their faces softened. Their lips turned upward. They were laughing!

This is what happened when people looked at Little.

"It's OK! We have twenty-five grandchildren!" said the man. "He is just adorable!"

Everyone started laughing.

Except Emma.

This was the worst dinner ever.

"Emma Bemma! Watch may!" Little shouted.

He picked up the purple crayon. He took a big bite.

"Kayons for dinna!" he yelled.

As Mommy swept the crayon from Little's mouth, it hit Emma. Little couldn't do big-kid things. Yet he was somehow a star of the dinner. That's how she decided on her plan for the next day.

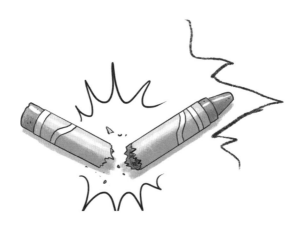

CHAPTER 6

Bam Bam and Boogers

Emma was building a gigantic sandcastle.

"Want to help?" she asked Wes. She was feeling sorry for how mean she had been.

"Yes!" Wes grabbed a bucket. He added more sand to the castle.

"It might even reach the clouds," Emma said as the creation grew.

"I'll dig a moat so enemies can't invade!" said Wes. He started to carve a deep pathway around the castle.

Then Little toddled over.

"Do not touch it!" warned Emma. But Little never listened. He was going to knock it over.

Then she remembered her plan. Today she was going to be little!

Emma crouched down next to Little. She waddled next to him. The two of them went around and around the castle.

Then Little found a shovel. He picked it up.

"Bam Bam!" he shouted. He smashed the top right off of the castle. Emma picked up a bigger shovel.

"Bam Bam!" she yelled even louder. She knocked the rest of the castle over right into Wes's moat. Then she jumped on top of it. Little joined her.

Emma looked up, smiling. Being little was fun! That's when she saw Wes's face. He looked sad, like everyone had forgotten his birthday. Emma looked away. Her tummy felt swishy again.

* * *

After lunch, the big kids popped right into the ocean. Emma wasn't allowed to do that without a grown-up. Today she didn't mind. She was little, not middle. And little kids got to do stuff that Emma

Just Medium wasn't supposed to do anymore.

She sat down next to Little by the water.

Little stuck a finger up his nose. Emma did too. It was wet.

Little pulled his finger out. He rubbed a booger ball in his fingers. He popped it in his mouth.

"Yummy!" he said.

Emma poked her finger in farther. She put a wet booger on her tongue. It was slimy. She spit it into the sand.

"Want to play a game?" she asked Little. She did not want to pick her nose anymore.

"Thwow sand!" Little shouted.

"Ok…" Emma said. She looked around. She knew this was a no-no. But being little meant you could do things middles couldn't. Emma dug her fingers into the heavy, dark sand. She pulled up a fistful. She tossed it up in the air. Sand drops rained on their heads.

"Moaw moaw!" yelled Little. That was Little's

word for 'more'. Emma did it again.

Little jumped up and down. Emma did too. They laughed so much it was hard to breathe.

Behind her, Wes watched. He sat by himself. Emma pretended she didn't notice.

Then Emma filled up both hands with sand. She tossed as hard as she could. Just then, the wind blew in. The sand flew backwards.

"Oww!" cried Wes. "My eyes!" Mrs. Farber came running over. She brought Wes back to the towel. She poured water in his eyes.

All of a sudden being little was not fun.

"Emma Joan!" yelled Mommy from behind them. "What were you thinking?"

"Little told me to!" Emma tried.

"He's a baby!"

"He's not a baby!" protested Emma. But Little was reaching his arms out to Mommy.

"Up up!" he cried. Mommy scooped him up like

ice cream. He put his thumb into his mouth. He looked down at Emma from Mommy's shoulder like a little bird in a nest.

"Up up!" echoed Emma, with her arms stretched high.

"Emma Bemma," Mommy sighed. "You're too big, I can't hold both of you."

Emma put her thumb in her mouth like Little did. It was salty. Mommy's face changed. She smiled but there were deep lines between her eyebrows.

"How about we hold hands, honey?" she said, gently. She reached down to take Emma's hand.

Emma yanked it away. She pulled her thumb out of her mouth. She marched away feeling very medium.

Emma sat down by the ocean and raked her feet in the sand. Tiny sand crabs appeared and then reburied themselves. Emma wanted to hide with them. Nothing was going right.

Suddenly she was swept up in the air.

"Lucky me, I found someone just the right size for

a toss in the water!" shouted Dad. Emma couldn't control herself from laughing.

Dad threw Emma into the gentle waves.

"You too, Wes the Best!" he called out to Wes who was still sitting with his Mom. Wes ran down to the water.

As the two middles took turns being launched into the ocean, just medium didn't seem so bad after all.

CHAPTER 7

Matthew the Middle

That night, Emma cuddled with Emmaphant. Then Dad came in. He sat down on her bed. He didn't sing a song. He didn't want to play a game. Was she in trouble? Emma pulled her covers up to her shoulders.

"Emma, Mommy and I noticed you're acting out of character on this vacation," he said. He looked kind of sad.

Emma nodded even though she wasn't sure what 'character' meant.

"This vacation isn't going so good," she said. A bubble was growing in her throat.

"You know, trying new things is great if you're doing them for the right reasons. But if you're doing those things to try to be someone you're not, that can be an uncomfortable fit."

Emma squinted her eyes. She thought for a second.

"Like a hermit crab whose shell is too small?" she asked.

"Exactly!" Dad said. He looked relieved.

"Remember, I was a middle too," he said.

"Really?" Emma couldn't believe Dad was ever a kid at all.

"Yes! I still am. Aunt Silly is my older sister. And Aunt Busy is my younger sister. I'm Matthew the Middle."

"Did you sometimes want to be in a different order?" asked Emma.

"Of course! Aunt Silly was really bossy and Aunt Busy whined all the time. Those two were so noisy I didn't think anyone would ever listen to me. But now your aunts are my best friends in the world."

Emma thought this over. She could not imagine Big or Little being her best friends. Or could she?

"I know it can be tough to be in between," Dad said. "But I think someday you may find it can be the sweetest spot, like the center of a jelly donut."

"I don't like jelly!" said Emma. She thought for a second. "How about the cream in an Oreo?"

Dad laughed. "Exactly," he said. "Without the cream, what would happen?"

"It would fall apart?"

"That's right. And it would be a pretty boring cookie, too. Remember, there are very special things about being right where you are."

"Like what?"

"Well, what do you think?"

"I can speak Spanish," said Emma, "and Little can't even speak English!"

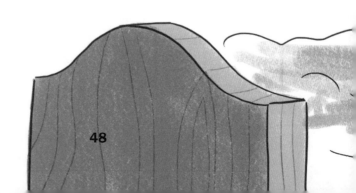

"Right!"

"And Big is too heavy to throw in the ocean?"

"Right. And Little can't even swim yet. You were little once too. And soon, you'll be big. But right now you've got the best of both worlds."

Emma thought about that for a minute.

"Dad?" Emma asked. "Why is my nickname Emma Bemma? Is it because I'm just medium and not big or little?"

"Oh Emma, of course not! You know how I love to rhyme. But we can change it if you'd like. How about Magnificent Medium? Marvelous Middle, M…"

"I know," said Emma, interrupting. "Emma Excelente! That's Spanish for Emma the Excellent."

"Done! Just remember, no matter what your nickname, you're always the best Emma you could be."

Then Dad added, "Now get some sleep. You need energy for your favorite day tomorrow…"

"Creature Cruise!" Emma shouted as she

remembered.

"Yes! And that's another special thing about you. You love ocean animals!"

Emma knew Dad was right. After he gave her a kiss and said good night, Emma dove into a dream filled with waving crabs, snapping lobsters and rainbow fish dancing in a circle, calling, "Emma Excelente!"

CHAPTER 8

Emma Excelente

"It's a very special boat trip. You get to touch lots of sea animals," Emma explained to Little and Baby Beth as their families boarded the Creature Cruise boat. Little was pulling Mommy the wrong way. Baby Beth squirmed in Mrs. Farber's arms. It was hard for little kids to understand. It was even harder for them to be patient.

"What color do you think the Creature Cruise t-shirt will be this year?" wondered Wes.

"I hope its green!" exclaimed Emma, looking down at her yellow Creature Cruise t-shirt. She was so excited she didn't care that it came out "gween."

"I'd rather go on a real fishing trip," Sara

announced. She and Big were trailing behind the group.

"Yeah, me too," echoed Big.

"Last year you wore your Creature Cruise t-shirt all month long!" Emma said.

"I'm double digits now, Emma Bemma," Big answered in the voice he used to sound grown-up. Emma imagined dark clouds forming over her perfect day.

Then she looked up at the sky. The sun was as yellow as her t-shirt. The sky was clear as Special's fish bowl. Emma looked back at Big. He had his sweatshirt hood over his eyes. He couldn't even see these things. He probably couldn't see at all.

Emma decided she wasn't going to let Big ruin her special day.

The boat slowly pulled out of the harbor. Wes and Emma moved to the back. They peered over the railing. Water bubbles formed a pathway behind them. Emma smiled to herself. It was good to be herself again.

In a few minutes, the boat dropped anchor.

"It's time!" said Emma. She couldn't wait for what was coming next.

But before she could get all the way from the back of the boat to where the captain was pulling up the net, a group of kids rushed in front of her. Emma was blocked. She knew there were critters of all shapes and sizes just ahead but she couldn't see anything!

"Let me in!" she cried. Nobody budged. She couldn't squeeze through any which way. Emma was stuck in the middle, again!

Emma could hear the captain showing other kids the sea creatures. One by one, he went through the crowd. Still, no turn for Emma. She was trying to be patient. It was getting harder.

Finally, the captain got closer. He was walking towards Emma. He held the biggest spider crab she had ever seen! Emma reached out to touch it. Then, he walked right past her to Big and Sara! Emma's jaw fell open. Not fair!

Sara shook her head. Then Big did too.

Emma gasped. They weren't even going to touch the crab! If being big meant missing out on what you liked because you were just a copycat, then Emma definitely didn't want to be big.

Still, no matter how patient she was, the captain wasn't noticing her. Emma tried to focus on the good parts of being medium. Instead it just meant she was missing out again.

As the yucky feelings washed over Emma, she clenched her fists together. Not one thing had changed this vacation no matter how hard she'd tried.

Then, Emma's eyes locked on Baby Beth. Aha! There was one thing she hadn't attempted yet.

Emma dropped down to her knees. She started to crawl. There was more space way down here! She could weave through everyone's legs. Being a baby was so obvious. Why hadn't she thought of it before?

Emma got closer and closer to the critter net. She saw the creatures' claws and legs waving about. She could almost touch them!

OUCH!

Emma looked up. The captain had stepped on her hand.

"Well, what's a big girl like you doing down there?" he said.

Emma's face was suddenly boiling. She stood up to her full height. She wanted to run away.

She turned around. Someone was standing in her way.

"Don't give up yet, Emma," said Wes. She realized he'd been right there all along.

So Emma took a deep breath, just like Mommy would. She turned back to the Captain.

"Would this little one like a turn?" he was saying

to Little. He was passing a hermit crab to Little. Little would crush it!

Little grabbed one of the crab's claws. He dangled the crab over the deck. He was going to drop it!

Emma squeezed through the crowd. She swooped in. She caught it just in time. PHEW. She cradled the creature in her hand. His claws tickled her palm.

Then Little reached his pinky finger out. He pet the crab.

"Nice job Little!" Emma cheered.

Mommy was smiling at Emma with her mouth and her eyes.

"Nice catch there," said the captain, "you seem to know a lot about crabs."

"Yes, they can live in the sea and on the land! They have the best of both worlds," said Emma. Dad nodded at her.

"Well, you're just the person we're looking for to help. We need to put these creatures in the tank."

Emma beamed. She followed the captain to the tank. Then she glanced back. Wes was looking at her.

"I'll be right there," she said. She ran back to Wes.

"Come on!" she said, grabbing his hand. Emma pulled her friend through the crowd.

"My friend is great with creatures too. Can he help?"

The captain handed Emma and Wes two big lobsters.

All the kids gathered around to watch as they lowered the lobsters carefully into the tank.

When they finished, Emma went to an open spot at the front of the boat. She looked down at the water. She pictured all the creatures living there. She thought of her own favorite fish at home.

The water started to ripple. Little circles formed.

SPLASH! A fish jumped out. Its little fin moved. He was waving! Another one jumped out, then another.

"Oh, they do that sometimes when they're feeding," said one of the women who worked on the boat.

Emma smiled to herself. She knew better.

CHAPTER 9

Just Emma!

The next day it was time to go home. They said goodbye to the Farbers one by one.

Then Mrs. Farber picked up Baby Beth. She held her out to Emma.

"I'm ready?" Emma asked. But she knew the answer. She cradled Baby Beth carefully. She kissed her dumpling cheeks. She sniffed her vanilla smell. When she handed baby Beth back to Mrs. Farber, she gave the baby a special crab wave goodbye.

Emma turned to Wes. She gave him a tight hug. He squeezed her back.

"I'm always your friend," said Wes.

"I know," Emma said. "You're Wes the Best."

When Emma got to the car, she saw who was driving.

"We're mixing things up around here!" Mommy said, smiling as she put her hands on the steering wheel.

Emma scrambled over Big's seat to get to her middle spot.

"Hold on Ms. Excelente, you are sitting over here, right behind me!" said Mommy, pointing to her booster at the window seat.

"That's Big's spot," said Emma.

"From now on, everyone gets a turn in the middle."

"But I don't fit there!" whined Big.

"Make it work," said Dad. He was not using his special voice. Big climbed into the middle without a word.

Emma buckled into her roomy new seat. All of the empty space around her felt funny. She moved her legs back and forth. She couldn't even see Mommy from this spot. Little was far away on the other side. Was he singing the ABC's or *Row Row Row Your Boat*? She looked at Big. He did not have his iPad. Dad had zipped it up tight in the suitcase. He was folded up like origami in the middle.

Emma smiled to herself. Big's legs were longer than hers. And someday hers would grow longer.

"Hey," Emma said, tapping Big. "Want to switch?"

"Yeah!" he said.

Emma asked Mommy to pull the car over. Big and Emma swapped places. "Gracias," Big whispered with a little smile.

"De nada," said Emma. "That means *you're welcome* in Spanish."

Dad reached back. He squeezed Emma's hand. Emma took a deep breath. She listened to Little's new song.

"Cwayons, cwayons...red and bwu!"

"And green!" added Emma. And this time it came out 'green'.

Then Emma noticed Mommy looking at her in the rearview mirror. She could see the middle best from her spot. She winked. Emma winked back.

"Ok, let's go!" Dad shouted as Mommy started the car.

"Let's go!" Emma sang back.

"Let's start the show!" joined in the whole family, even Big.

Emma settled into her seat for the rest of the ride home. The middle wasn't just medium. It was just right. And she was Emma, just who she should be.

THE END

Andrea Chalon

ABOUT THE AUTHOR

Laura Wiltse Prior went from creating tales starring "Laura the Great" in her dad's studio office, to crafting short stories when she was supposed to be working in a business office, to writing books for kids in her very own office (well, one she shares with her son's Xbox). She loves reading anything and everything, sneaking cookie dough from the mixing bowl and playing tennis. When she isn't writing, Laura's ferrying her kids around, hiking with her dog Cody, or hanging with Casper the cat. She lives in Connecticut with her husband and three kids, the inspiration for her authentic family stories.